D1492189

3 8002 02239 786 5

COVENTRY LIBRARIES
WITHDRAWN
FOR SALE

The Mystery of the

HAUNTED FARM

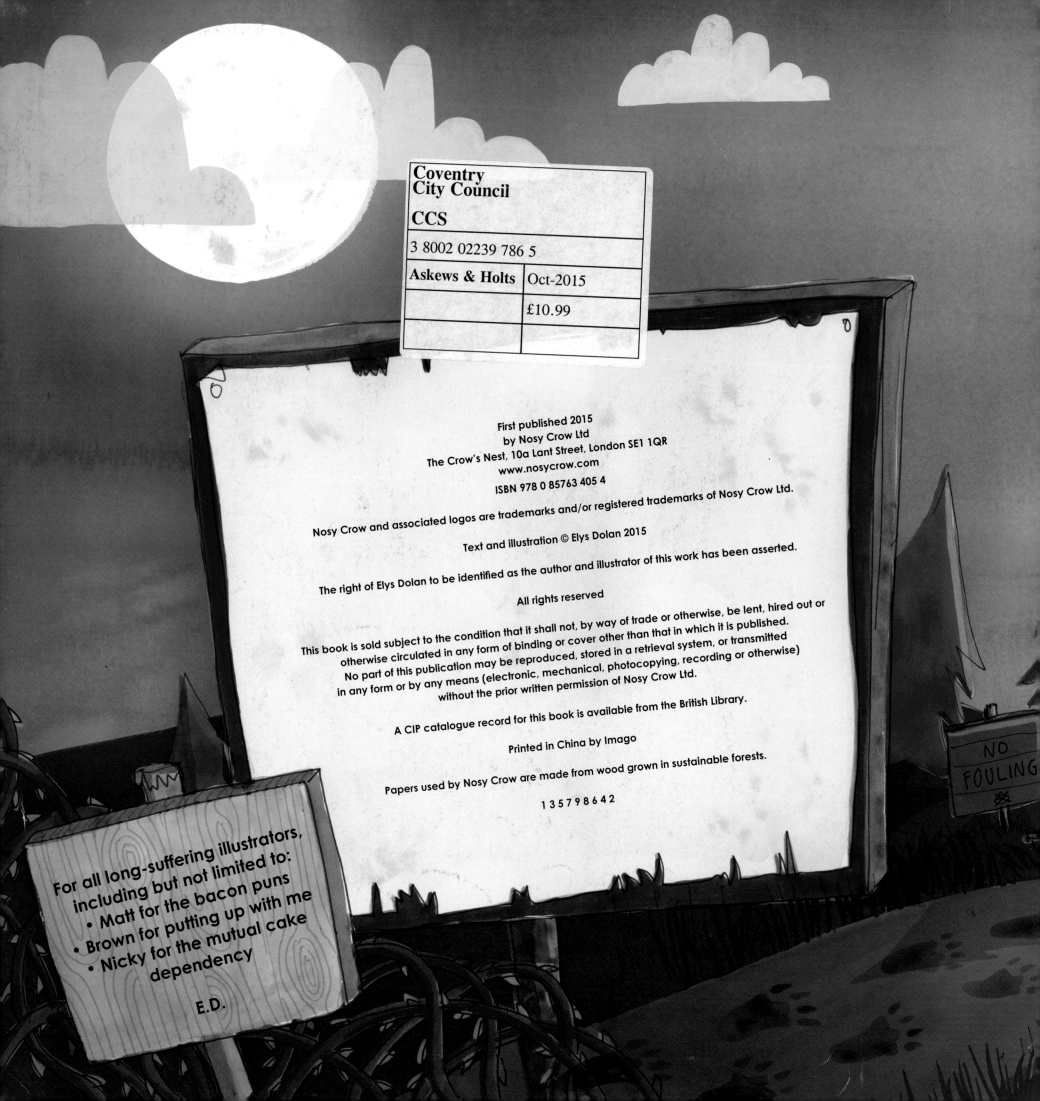

Coventry City Council

CCS

3 8002 02239 786 5

Askews & Holts	Oct-2015
	£10.99

First published 2015
by Nosy Crow Ltd
The Crow's Nest, 10a Lant Street, London SE1 1QR
www.nosycrow.com

ISBN 978 0 85763 405 4

Nosy Crow and associated logos are trademarks and/or registered trademarks of Nosy Crow Ltd.

Text and illustration © Elys Dolan 2015

The right of Elys Dolan to be identified as the author and illustrator of this work has been asserted.

All rights reserved

This book is sold subject to the condition that it shall not, by way of trade or otherwise, be lent, hired out or
otherwise circulated in any form of binding or cover other than that in which it is published.
No part of this publication may be reproduced, stored in a retrieval system, or transmitted
in any form or by any means (electronic, mechanical, photocopying, recording or otherwise)
without the prior written permission of Nosy Crow Ltd.

A CIP catalogue record for this book is available from the British Library.

Printed in China by Imago

Papers used by Nosy Crow are made from wood grown in sustainable forests.

1 3 5 7 9 8 6 4 2

For all long-suffering illustrators,
including but not limited to:
• Matt for the bacon puns
• Brown for putting up with me
• Nicky for the mutual cake
dependency

E.D.

NO
FOULING

Down on the farm, something wasn't quite right . . .

. . . and Farmer Greg had had enough.

HONK! HONK!

These Ghost-Hunters were even equipped with the latest Scare-o-Meter, the Phantom Finder 5000. In no time at all, they were on their way.

The Ghost-Hunters went straight to the pond which seemed to have a bit of a zombie duck problem . . .

. . . but the Phantom Finder 5000 did not register any paranormal activity. So they went to investigate the farmhouse instead.

It looked as if the barn had been invaded by some terrifyingly gooey supernatural creatures . . .

... but the Phantom Finder 5000 STILL registered zero. The Ghost-Hunters were baffled – how could there be so many scary things around without the Phantom Finder 5000 picking anything up? The only place left to look was the vegetable patch.

And it was while they were rooting around the gruesome greens that they found the clue they'd been looking for. Everything led to the mysterious chicken coop on the hill.

And in the vegetable patch, they also found Farmer Greg.

In all their years in the business, the Ghost-hunters had never seen an underground fear factory like *this* before. But *why* would the animals build such a thing and pretend to be ghosts and ghouls?

But then something very strange started to happen to Farmer Greg . . .

Farmer Greg turned into a . . .

The Ghost-Hunters knew exactly what to do.

And the training was a success.

From then on, every full moon Greg was a very good wolf . . .

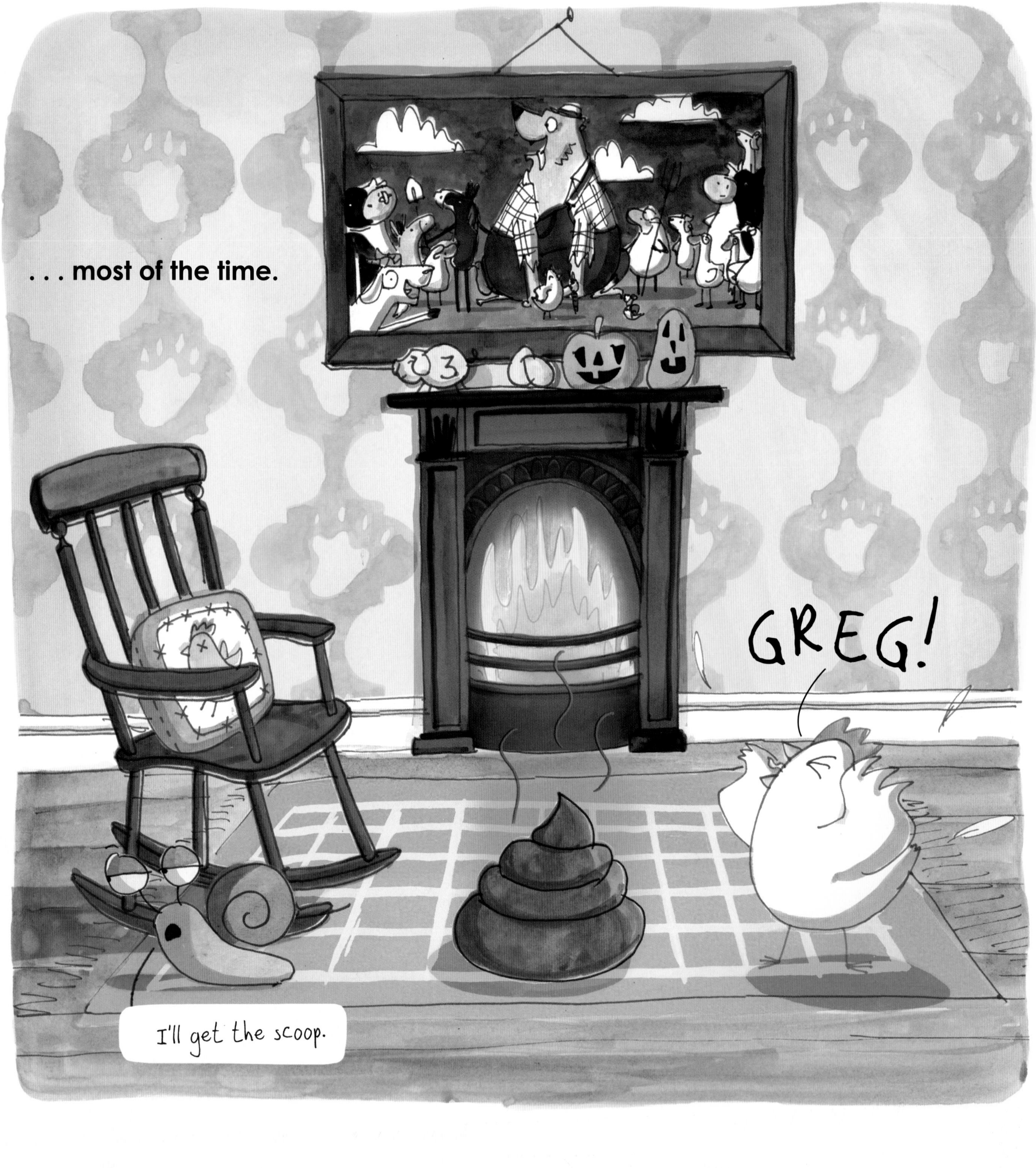
. . . most of the time.
GREG!
I'll get the scoop.